Hafro and the Ghostly, Ghastly Rubbish

Dear ori

Best wishes and
enjoy the Story
with love.

Peggy Flo.
x.

Peggy Flo

Charles Barry

MAPLE
PUBLISHERS

Hafro and the Ghostly, Ghastly Rubbish

Author: Peggy Flo

Copyright © Peggy Flo (2022)

Illustrated by Charles Barry

The right of Peggy Flo to be identified as author of this work has been asserted by the author in accordance with section 77 and 78 of the Copyright, Designs and Patents Act 1988.

First Published in 2022

ISBN: 978-1-915796-09-7 (Paperback)
978-1-915796-15-8 (Hardback)
978-1-915796-16-5 (Ebook)

Book layout by:

White Magic Studios

www.whitemagicstudios.co.uk

Published by:

Maple Publishers

Fairbourne Drive

Atterbury,

Milton Keynes

MK10 9RG

www.maplepublishers.com

A CIP catalogue record for this title is available from the British Library.

A big thank you to

Samuel Perry, aged 9, year 5

for reading the book and loving the ending

Hafro stretched out in the sunshine,

The pillow he used was a log,

A strange looking creature - not unlike a hare,

But he also resembles a frog.

His home in the woodland was peaceful,

He looked up at the trees and the sky,

There were beautiful flowers around him,

The tweeting of birds flying by.

In the distance he heard a faint rumbling,

A sound he had not heard before,

He jumped to his feet, tripped over the log,

And rolled like a ball on the floor.

He came to a stop near a pathway,

The rumbling noise was quite near,

He then heard the clatter and breaking of glass,

This commotion would soon become clear.

The pathway leads up to an opening,

Where woodland folk meet in the day,

Hafro hopped up the path to see what was there,

As a bright coloured van pulled away.

What he saw made him shout out in horror,

There were bottles and cans piled high,

Squashing the colourful flowers,

He was sure he could hear them all cry.

Hafro hurried to find his friend Blipso,

He was saddened and deeply annoyed,

They must warn woodland folk of the dangers,

The clearing they all should avoid.

Blipso was polishing conkers,

As Hafro hopped up at a pace,

"Blipso you're needed, we'll raise the alarm,

The clearing's a dreadful disgrace".

Hafro explained the dilemma,

As they found woodland folk one by one.

The two didn't stop until all had been warned.

Next, what to do - should be done?

They both came up close to the clearing,

And didn't know quite what to say,

The pile had grown higher, more

bottles and cans,

A scene of such utter dismay!

Near the edge of the pile and seemingly pleased,

Was the infamous Thorny Nosed Leech,

He was grabbing at bottles to throw them about,

And anything else he could reach.

The mess in this beautiful woodland,

Was enough to make anyone curse,

Hafro was sure the van would come back,

And the pile could only get worse.

The Thorny Nosed Leech didn't listen,

When Hafro asked "please can you stop"?

He scattered the rubbish all over the place,

In the river it fell with a plop!

This had to be cleared up so quickly,

In case animals trod on the glass,

It was sharp and nastily jagged,

Not easy to see in the grass.

His friends came to see what had happened,

As Hafro then thought up a plan,

A brilliant idea to clear up the mess,

And stop future drops from the van.

Using plastic and pens from the rubbish,

They made signs that they placed all around,

The writing said "These woods are HAUNTED",

And they hammered them into the ground.

The woodland folk waited for nightfall,

They hid in the hollows and trees,

A wild ghostly noise drifted into the air,

Which was made by the whispering breeze.

Very soon they could hear the faint rumbling,

The van then came back into sight,

Before further rubbish was tipped on the ground,

Woodland folk would create such a fright.

Hafro wailed a loud haunting ghost cry,

"All spooks of the woodland are here,

We'll gather around you and swallow you up,

If you don't make this mess disappear".

The man with the van was so frightened,

He saw eyes peering out way up high,

The signs he soon read and realised at once,

There were ghosts that were waiting nearby.

Hafro groaned, the man tumbled over,

He fell to the floor with a crash,

Then jumped to his feet, scurried about

And cleared up the mess in a flash.

He left in a frenzy – so frightened,

The message he got very plain,

The rumbling silenced, peace was restored,

And guess what? He was not seen again.

They cheered, clapped and laughed at their victory,

So pleased no more plastic or tin,

It's all very simple and easy to do,

Just recycle it into a bin.

Hafro stopped for a moment and listened,

A faint cry for help he could hear,

It was coming from deep in the river,

At the edge they all gathered quite near.

Stuck in a clear plastic bottle,

Floating away out of reach,

Being chased by some fish and

long slimy eels,

Was the infamous Thorny Nosed Leech,

This world is just one of such beauty,

To be cherished, enjoyed every day,

Forests and oceans, animals too,

Let's love them and keep it this way.

Also in the Hafro Series;

Hafro And The Wicked Leech

Hafro And The Ghostly, Ghastly Rubbish

Hafro And The Drizmal Day

Hafro And The Pinkasnub

Hafro And The Brave Rescue

Lightning Source UK Ltd.
Milton Keynes UK
UKRC042358260223
417688UK00001B/4

* 9 7 8 1 9 1 5 7 9 6 0 9 7 *